Room Nine, Kindergarten Friends

Mrs.

Junie B. Jones

Richie Lucille

That Grace

Meanie Jim

Crybaby William

Paulie Allen Puffer

Jamal Hall

Ricardo

Roger

Charlotte

Lynnie

Laugh Out Loud with Junie B. Jones!

#1 *Junie B. Jones and the Stupid Smelly Bus*
#2 *Junie B. Jones and a Little Monkey Business*
#3 *Junie B. Jones and Her Big Fat Mouth*
#4 *Junie B. Jones and Some Sneaky Peeky Spying*
#5 *Junie B. Jones and the Yucky Blucky Fruitcake*
#6 *Junie B. Jones and That Meanie Jim's Birthday*
#7 *Junie B. Jones Loves Handsome Warren*
#8 *Junie B. Jones Has a Monster Under Her Bed*
#9 *Junie B. Jones Is Not a Crook*
#10 *Junie B. Jones Is a Party Animal*
#11 *Junie B. Jones Is a Beauty Shop Guy*
#12 *Junie B. Jones Smells Something Fishy*
#13 *Junie B. Jones Is (almost) a Flower Girl*
#14 *Junie B. Jones and the Mushy Gushy Valentime*
#15 *Junie B. Jones Has a Peep in Her Pocket*
#16 *Junie B. Jones Is Captain Field Day*
#17 *Junie B. Jones Is a Graduation Girl*
#18 *Junie B. Jones: First Grader (at last!)*
#19 *Junie B. Jones: Boss of Lunch*
#20 *Junie B. Jones: Toothless Wonder*
#21 *Junie B. Jones: Cheater Pants*
#22 *Junie B. Jones: One-Man Band*
#23 *Junie B. Jones: Shipwrecked*
#24 *Junie B. Jones: BOO . . . and I MEAN It!*
#25 *Junie B. Jones: Jingle Bells, Batman Smells! (P.S. So Does May.)*
#26 *Junie B. Jones: Aloha-ha-ha!*
#27 *Junie B. Jones: Dumb Bunny*
#28 *Junie B. Jones: Turkeys We Have Loved and Eaten (and Other Thankful Stuff)*
Junie B. Jones: Top-Secret Personal Beeswax: A Journal by Junie B. (and me!)
Junie B.'s Essential Survival Guide to School
Junie B. Jones: These Puzzles Hurt My Brain! Book
Junie B. Jones: Junie B. My Valentime

junie b. jones®
Is Not a Crook

by BARBARA PARK

illustrated by
Denise Brunkus

A STEPPING STONE BOOK™

Random House New York

This is a work of fiction. Names, characters, places, and incidents either are the product of the author's imagination or are used fictitiously. Any resemblance to actual persons, living or dead, events, or locales is entirely coincidental.

 Published in the United States by Random House Children's Books, a division of Random House LLC, a Penguin Random House Company, New York.

JunieBJones.com

Educators and librarians, for a variety of teaching tools, visit us at RHTeachersLibrarians.com

Library of Congress Cataloging-in-Publication Data
Park, Barbara.
Junie B. Jones is not a crook / by Barbara Park ; illustrated by Denise Brunkus.
p. cm. "A stepping stone book."
Summary: Junie B. Jones experiences glee while showing off her new furry mittens in kindergarten, but disaster strikes when they disappear from the playground.
ISBN 978-0-679-88342-5 (pbk.) — ISBN 978-0-679-98342-2 (lib. bdg.) —
ISBN 978-0-307-75475-2 (ebook)
[1. Mittens—Fiction. 2. Lost and found possessions—Fiction.
3. Honesty—Fiction. 4. Kindergarten—Fiction. 5. Schools—Fiction.]
I. Brunkus, Denise, ill. II. Title.
PZ7.P2197Jtx 1997 [Fic]—dc20 96-42542

Printed in the United States of America 59 58 57 56 55 54 53 52 51 50 49 48 47

This book has been officially leveled by using the F&P Text Level Gradient™ Leveling System.

Random House Children's Books supports the First Amendment and celebrates the right to read.

Contents

1
No Good Reason

My name is Junie B. Jones. The B stands for Beatrice. Except I don't like Beatrice. I just like B and that's all.

Here is a story for you.

It is called "Once Upon a Time My Grandfather Named Frank Miller Went to the Store and He Bought Me Some Mittens."

Once upon a time my grandfather named Frank Miller went to the store and he bought me some mittens. They are made out of black furry fur.

And guess what? It was not even my

birthday! Or Christmas! Or Valentine's Day! Plus the mittens were not even on sale!

Grampa Miller just bought them for no good reason! And that is the bestest reason I ever heard of!

That's how come I love that guy very much.

Plus also he can skip.

The end.

I like that story a real lot.

'Cause guess why?

I didn't even make it up, that's why!

That adventure actually happened to me! My grampa Miller really *did* buy me mittens for no good reason!

And they are gorgeous, I tell you!

When I first opened them, I got filled with glee.

Glee is when you run. And jump. And

skip. And laugh. And clap. And dance on top of the dining room table.

Then your mother takes you down from the table. And she carries you to your room for a *time-out.*

Time-outs kill the glee.

I wore my new mittens the whole entire morning. Plus also I wore them to afternoon kindergarten.

I wore them with my attractive winter jacket. Only it wasn't actually cold out. Only who even cares? 'Cause that outfit looked very beautiful together.

I showed my mittens to my bestest friend named Grace. Also, I showed them to a variety of strangers.

After I got to school, I held my hands over my head. And I runned all over the playground.

"LOOK, EVERYBODY! LOOK AT MY NEW MITTENS! MY GRAMPA FRANK MILLER BOUGHT THEM FOR NO GOOD REASON!"

I waved them all around in the air.

"HOW MANY CHILDREN SEE THESE LOVELY THINGS? RAISE YOUR HANDS," I hollered.

Nobody raised their hands.

"HOW MANY CHILDREN THINK THESE MITTENS ARE GORGEOUS? PLEASE COME FORWARD!" I yelled.

Nobody came forward.

I put my hands back down and walked to that Grace.

"I couldn't create any interest," I said very glum.

Only guess what? Just then, I spotted my other bestest friend named Lucille!

I ran my fastest to greet her.

"LUCILLE! LUCILLE! LOOK AT MY GORGEOUS NEW MITTENS! SEE THEM? THEY ARE MADE OUT OF BLACK FURRY FUR!"

Lucille petted them.

"My family has *lots* of fur," she said.

"My mother has a fur cape. And my aunt has a fur jacket. And my uncle has a fur hat. Plus my nanna just bought a brand-new mink coat. Only she can't wear it outside the house. Or else people will throw paint on her."

My mouth came all the way open.

"Why, Lucille? Why will people throw paint on your nanna?" I asked.

Lucille crossed her arms.

"Don't you know *anything,* Junie B. Jones? It's because people who love furry animals don't like them being made into coats for nannas."

Just then, I felt relief in me. 'Cause I'm not even a nanna, that's why. And besides, my mittens aren't even made out of *real* furry animals. They are made out of *fake* furry animals. And those kind don't even count.

All of a sudden, the bell rang for school.

I zoomed to my room like a speeding rocket.

'Cause guess why?

More people to show my mittens to!

That's why!

2
Fur Hands

I showed my mittens to my teacher.

Her name is Mrs.

She has another name, too. But I just like Mrs. and that's all.

"Feel them, Mrs.," I said. "Feel how soft they are."

I rubbed them on her face.

"Oooh, they *are* soft, Junie B.," she said. "Be sure and put them in your jacket pockets so they won't get lost, okay?"

I skipped very happy to my seat.

"Yeah, only I'm not even going to lose them," I said to just myself. "I am going to wear them right on my hands. The whole livelong day. 'Cause I love these guys, that's why."

I took off my attractive winter jacket. And sat down at my table.

Then I tapped on Lucille with my furry mittens.

"Hello. How are you today? I have fur hands. See them, Lucille? See my hands of fur?"

I flew them in the air.

"This is what fur hands look like when they're flying in the air," I said.

I waved hello.

"This is what fur hands look like when they're waving hello," I said.

Lucille did a frown.

"You're being annoying," she said.

That's how come I turned around. And I smiled at a boy named William.

"I have fur hands, William. See them? See my fur hands?"

I tapped on his head.

"This is what fur hands look like when they're tapping you on your head," I said.

Just then, I got up from my chair. And I skipped to my boyfriend named Ricardo.

I tickled him under the chin with my softy hands of fur.

"This is what fur hands look like when they're tickling you under your chin," I said.

Then I grinned and grinned. 'Cause that boy brings out the best in me. That's why.

Pretty soon, Mrs. saw me out of my seat.

She held my hand and marched me back to my table.

"This is how fur hands look when they're marching to my table," I said.

Mrs. plopped me in my chair.

Then she pulled off my fur hands. And she put them on her desk.

I did a sad sigh.

"That is how fur hands look when they're no longer in my possession," I whispered to just myself.

After that, I put my head on my desk.

And covered up with my arms.

And I didn't come out for a real long time.

3
Being Brownie

Mrs. said I could have my mittens back at recess.

I stared and stared at the clock. Then I tapped my fingers on my table. And I did loud breaths.

Lucille tattletaled on me.

"Junie B. keeps tapping her fingers and making loud breaths! And I can't even concentrate on my work!" she grouched.

Mrs. came to my table.

"Hello. How are you today?" I said kind

of nervous. "I am fine. Except I don't actually have my mittens."

She tapped her foot real fast.

That was not a good sign, I think.

Only guess what? Just then, the bell rang for recess!

"OH BOY!" I yelled. "OH BOY! OH BOY! 'CAUSE NOW I CAN HAVE MY MITTENS BACK! RIGHT, MRS.? RIGHT? RIGHT?"

I zoomed to her desk and put them on my hands.

Then I rubbed those softy things all over my cheeks.

"It's good to be with you again," I whispered into their fur.

After that, I put on my attractive winter jacket. And I skipped outside with my friends.

Me and tattletale Lucille and that Grace play horses together at recess.

I am Brownie. Lucille is Blackie. And that Grace is Yellowie.

"I'M YELLOWIE!" shouted that Grace.

"I'M BLACKIE!" shouted Lucille.

"I'M BROWNIE!" I shouted.

Only just then, I looked at my mittens.

I did a frown.

'Cause there was a little bit of a problem here, I think.

"Yeah, only how can I even be Brownie? 'Cause my horse paws are black. And so I am two different colors, apparently."

Lucille and that Grace did frowns, too.

"Hmm," said that Grace.

"Hmm," said Lucille.

"Hmm," I said.

Just then, that Grace clapped her hands

together very excited. "*I* know, Junie B.! Today you and Lucille can *trade!* Today *Lucille* can be Brownie! And *you* can be Blackie! And so that way your horse paws will be the right color!"

Me and Lucille looked and looked at that girl. 'Cause what kind of crazy idea was that?

I did a huffy breath.

"Yeah, only how can I even be *Blackie* when I am already *Brownie,* Grace?" I said. "I have been Brownie for my whole entire career. You can't just go *changing,* you know."

"Yeah, Grace. You can't just go *changing,*" said Lucille.

That Grace looked embarrassed at herself. "Oh yeah...What was I thinking?" she said very mumbling.

After that, all of us sat down in the grass. And we tapped on our chins.

We thinked and thinked and thinked.

Then—all of a sudden—my whole face lighted up.

"Hey! I thought of it! I thought of it! I know 'zactly what to do!" I shouted.

I jumped up.

"Start again, Grace! Say your name again! Say that you are Yellowie!"

That Grace looked curious at me.

"I'm Yellowie," she said.

I pointed to Lucille.

"I'm Blackie," she said next.

I spinned around real joyful.

"I'M BROWNIE!" I shouted. "ONLY GUESS WHAT? YESTERDAY MY GRAMPA BROWNIE BOUGHT ME BLACK FURRY MITTENS! AND SO

THAT IS HOW COME I AM TWO DIFFERENT COLORS, APPARENTLY!"

After that, all of us did high fives. And we started playing horses.

We galloped. And trotted. And snorted. And snuffled.

Only too bad for me. 'Cause the sun kept on beating down on my horse head. And I got drippity inside my attractive winter jacket.

"I am going to die from heat perspiration," I said.

That's how come I trotted over to a tree. And I took off all my stuff.

First I took off my attractive winter jacket. Then I took off my furry black mittens. And I piled them in a careful pile.

After that, I galloped away to find my horse friends. And we played and played.

Pretty soon, Mrs. blew her loud whistle.

That means the end of recess.

"COMING!" shouted Yellowie.

"COMING!" shouted Blackie.

"COMING!" I shouted.

Then I hurried up back to the tree to get my stuff.

Only guess what?

I saw something very terrible there, that's what!

And it's called *HEY!!! SOMEBODY STOLED MY MITTENS!!!!!*

4
No Teddy Backpack

I runned all around the tree.

"911! 911! 911!" I hollered. "SOMEBODY STOLED THEM! SOMEBODY STOLED MY MITTENS!"

Mrs. came very quick.

"THEY STOLED THEM! THEY STOLED MY MITTENS! 911!" I shouted some more.

Mrs. bended down next to me. "*Who,* Junie B.? Who stole them?" she asked.

"A stealer, that's who! A stealer stoled them! And so what kind of school is this? 'Cause I didn't even know there was crooks at this place!"

Mrs. said calm down my voice.

"Yeah, only I can't even calm it down that good. 'Cause I am heartsick, that's why."

Heartsick is the grown-up word for when your heart is sick.

I looked at the ground real sad. "Now all I have left is my dumb attractive jacket."

Mrs. picked it up. Then she holded my hand. And me and her started to walk.

"You and I are going to the office," she told me.

I quick tried to get my hand away from her.

"No, Mrs.! I'm not allowed to go there!

Mother said if I get sended to the office one more time, I will get *grounded, young lady.*"

Tears came in my eyes.

"*Grounded, young lady,* is when I have to stay on my own ground," I said. "Plus also I can go on the rug."

Mrs. smiled. "I'm not taking you to the principal's office to *punish* you, Junie B.," she said. "I'm taking you to find your mittens."

I did a gasp.

"Principal?" I asked very shocked. "Principal stoled my mittens?"

Mrs. laughed real loud.

"No, Junie B. He didn't steal your mittens. The office is where the Lost and Found is located."

After that, she took my hand again. And we hurried up to the office.

There is a grouchy typing lady at that place.

I am not fond of her.

"Junie B. needs to look through the Lost and Found," Mrs. told her. "Please send her back to class when she's finished."

Then Mrs. went back to Room Nine and left me there all by myself.

The typing lady looked over the counter at me.

I did a gulp.

"Yeah, only I'm not even bad today," I explained very nervous. "Somebody stoled my mittens. And that is the end of my tale."

The typing lady kept on looking at me. She didn't say any words.

Sweat came on my head.

"Whew...it's warmish in here, isn't it?" I said.

Just then, I heard a door open.

It was Principal!

He was coming out of his office!

I jumped up and down at his sight. 'Cause I know that guy very good!

"Principal! Look! Look! It's me! It's Junie B. Jones! My mittens got stoled on the playground! And so Mrs. brought me here to get them! So just hand them over and I will be on my way...no questions asked."

Principal looked funny at me. Then he went to the closet and pulled out a big box.

"This is the Lost and Found, Junie B.," he explained. "Anytime that someone finds something that's been lost, they bring it here. And we put it in this box."

"How come?" I asked. "How come they bring it here instead of taking it home? 'Cause one time I found a nickel in the street. And Daddy said I could put it in my bank. 'Cause *finding* isn't the same thing as *stealing*. Right, Principal? Finding is a *lucky duck*."

Principal laughed a little bit.

"Well, finding a nickel in the street is different, Junie B.," he said. "For one thing, it would be almost impossible to discover who the owner of the nickel really was. And for another thing, losing a nickel isn't really a big deal. But when someone loses something *personal*—like mittens, for instance—well, that's a *very* big deal. And so if someone else *finds* the mittens, they can bring them to the Lost and Found, and the owner can get them back."

He smiled.

"And that makes everyone happy, Junie B.," he said. "The owner is happy because she has her mittens back. And the person who found them is happy because she's done a good deed."

He pointed to a piece of paper taped on the box.

"See this? This is a poem the third grade wrote about the Lost and Found. It says:

> *"If you find stuff,*
> *Bring it in.*
> *All day long,*
> *You'll wear a grin."*

I did a frown.

"Yeah, only here's the problem. I didn't *lose* my mittens. They got stoled on *purpose.* And so no one will bring them in and wear a grin, probably."

Principal raised up his eyebrows. "Well,

you never know, Junie B. Why don't you look in there and see?"

He opened up the box for me.

That's when my eyes got big and wide.

'Cause it was filled with the wonderfulest items I ever saw!

There were sweaters! And sweatshirts! And baseball caps! And gloves! And balls! And a lunchbox! And a scarf! And sunglasses! And a watch with Mickey Mouse on it!

Also, there was a backpack that looked like a teddy bear!

"OOOOH! I ALWAYS WANTED ONE OF THESE!" I hollered real thrilled.

I put it on my back and skipped around the office.

"How does it look back there?" I asked.

Principal runned after me.

If you find stuff,
Bring it in.
All day long,
You'll wear a grin.

He took the teddy off my back. And put it back in the box.

"We're looking for your *mittens*, remember?"

Just then, I felt upset again. 'Cause I almost forgot about those furry guys, that's why.

"Oh, yeah...my mittens," I said real glum.

I looked through the box some more.

"They're not here," I said. "My mittens are gone forever and ever, I think."

I did a sad sigh.

Then I picked up the teddy backpack again.

"Maybe I will take *this* instead," I said. "'Cause this teddy backpack will ease my pain, I believe."

Principal said no.

"How come?" I asked. "'Cause the owner doesn't even want it anymore, I bet. Her mother already bought her a new teddy backpack, probably. And so this one is just going to go to waste."

Principal stood me up and turned me to the door.

That meant I am leaving, I think.

"Come back tomorrow and look for your mittens again," he said.

I talked real fast.

"Yeah, only I just remembered something. I used to have a teddy backpack just like that one, maybe. Only then I lost it, probably. And so I better take that one home with me. Or else my mother might be mad."

Principal walked me to the door. He faced me down the hall.

"Good-bye, Junie B.," he said.

I hanged my head real disappointed.

'Cause guess why?

Good-bye means *no teddy backpack*.

5
Gargling and Scribbling

Room Nine is way far from Principal's office.

I had to stop at the water fountain. Or else I might not make it.

I pressed the water button with my thumb.

Then I puckered up my lips. And I sucked the water in.

I didn't even put my mouth on the spout. 'Cause there's lip dirt on that thing of course.

I sloshed the water all around in my cheeks.

Then I bended my head way back. And I did some gargles.

I can gargle very perfect. Except I can't keep the water in my actual mouth.

It runned out the sides and dribbled on the floor.

I splashed in it with my toe.

That's when I saw something very wonderful down there.

"Hey! It's one of those pens that writes four different colors!" I said.

I quick picked it up and pushed the little red button on the top.

A red pen popped out the bottom.

I scribbled red scribble all over my hand.

"Wowie wow wow! I *love* this thing!" I said.

After that, I pushed the green button and scribbled green scribble. And I pushed the blue button and scribbled blue scribble. Plus also I pushed the black button and scribbled black scribble.

"This pen makes scribbling a pleasure," I said.

I put it in my pocket and started skipping to Room Nine.

Only too bad for me. 'Cause all of a sudden, I remembered about the Lost and Found.

I stopped.

"Oh no. I wish I didn't even remember about that," I said. "Now I have to take my pen to the Lost and Found. Or else I won't wear a grin."

I did a frown. 'Cause something didn't make sense here, that's why.

"Yeah, only I was already *wearing* a grin," I said. "I weared a grin as soon as I *saw* this wonderful thing. And so taking it to the office will only make me sad."

I tapped on my chin.

"Hmm. Maybe Principal is a little mixed up about this," I said to just myself. "I'm pretty sure I will be happier if I keep it.

"And here's another thing I am thinking. I am thinking whoever owned this pen didn't even take good care of it. So I will give it a good home. And so what can be a gooder deed than that?"

I took it out of my pocket and looked at it.

"Plus this even makes sense. 'Cause first I got my mittens stolen. And then I couldn't have the teddy backpack. And so keeping this pen is fair and square."

All of a sudden, my whole face lighted up. 'Cause I just thought of a *different* poem, that's why!

And it is called *Finders keepers, losers weepers!*

"Finders keepers, losers weepers!" I said real thrilled. "Finders keepers, losers weepers!"

Then I jumped up and down very happy. 'Cause everybody says that! And so *Finders keepers* is really the rule, I bet!

After that, I put my pen back in my pocket.

And I skipped the rest of the way to Room Nine.

6
My Grampa's Wallet

I kept my pen in my pocket the whole rest of the day.

I didn't want people to see it. Or else they might tattletale to Mrs. And she would make me take it to the Lost and Found.

I behaved myself very good. 'Cause I didn't want to 'tract 'tention, that's why.

I kept my hand in my pocket so my pen would not fall out.

Also, I kept thinking about my mittens.

’Cause I still missed those furry guys.

I put my head down on my table.

“Maybe my grampa Miller might buy me some *more* furry mittens,” I whispered. “’Cause that would be a perfect solution, I think.”

I raised up my head.

“Hey, yeah! Then I would have wonderful new mittens, *plus* a wonderful new pen. And so what more can a girl ask for? That’s what I’d like to know!”

I sat up in my chair and tapped on Lucille.

“Guess what, Lucille? Maybe my grampa Frank Miller might buy me some new mittens. And then all my troubles will be over.”

Lucille said *whoop-de-do* for me.

“I know it is *whoop-de-do*,” I said real

thrilled. “And so, thank you for your support.”

After school, me and my bestest friend named Grace rode the bus together.

I runned home from my corner like a speedy bullet.

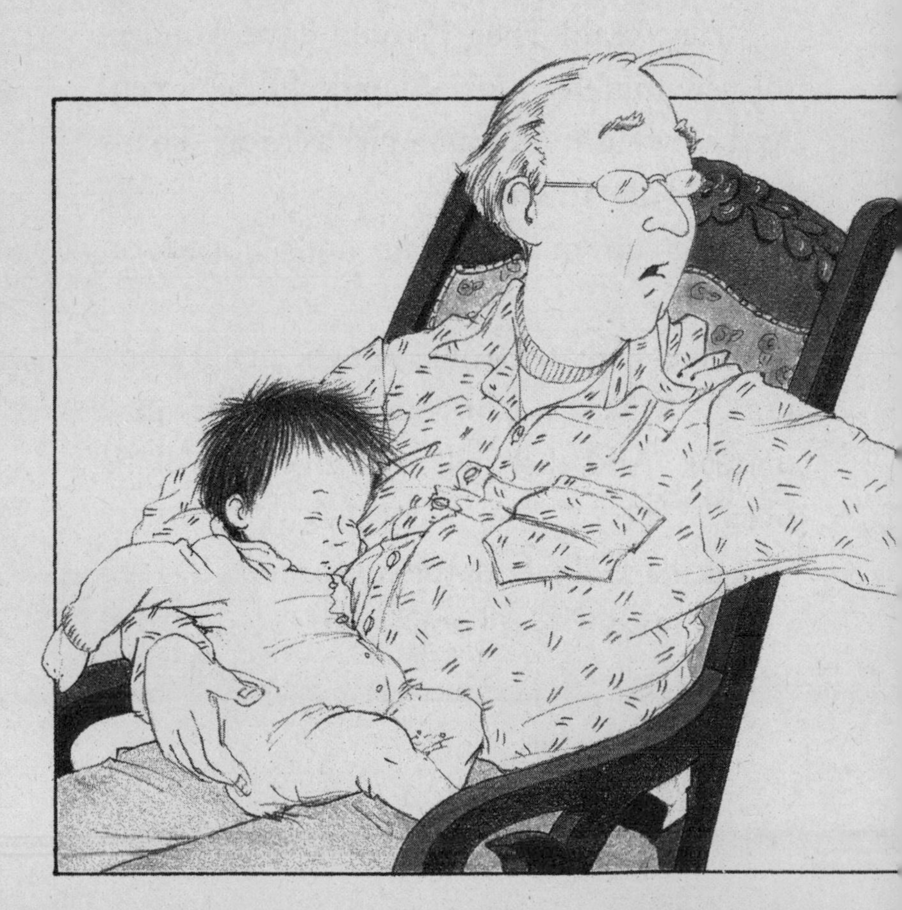

My grampa Frank Miller was babysitting my brother named Ollie.

"GRAMPA FRANK MILLER! GRAMPA FRANK MILLER! WE GOTTA GO TO THE MITTEN STORE! WE GOTTA GO TO THE MITTEN STORE!" I hollered real loud.

Grampa Frank Miller was in the living room rocking Ollie.

He looked funny at me.

"Go *where?*" he asked.

"TO THE MITTEN STORE! TO THE MITTEN STORE! WE GOTTA GO TO THE MITTEN STORE!"

I pulled on his hand.

"GET UP! GET UP! LET'S GET A WIGGLE ON!"

Grampa Miller looked confused at me.

That's how come I had to sit down. And I told him what happened at school.

"Someone stoled my mittens," I said. "They stoled them while I was being Brownie. And I didn't even know there were crooks at that place."

Grampa Frank Miller shook his head very sad.

"I guess you can find crooks almost anywhere, honey," he said.

"I know it," I told him. "That's how come I'm never going to see those furry guys again. And so you and me have to go to the mitten store."

I felt in his back pocket. Then I danced around real thrilled.

"Hurray!" I shouted. "Hurray for your big fat wallet! 'Cause you got cash in there. Right, Grampa? Right? Right?"

Grampa Frank Miller laughed.

"Yes, I do. I've got cash all right," he said. "But I'm afraid we won't be able to buy you more mittens. The mittens I bought you were the only furry ones they had left. I bought the very last pair."

Just then, all the happy went right out of me. 'Cause I didn't actually count on this terrible development.

"Yeah, only we *have* to, Grampa. We *have* to buy more furry mittens. Or else what will I even do?"

Grampa Miller ruffled my hair.

"Did you look in the Lost and Found at school?" he asked.

I did a sad breath. "Yeah, only that dumb thing doesn't work that good. 'Cause people don't always turn stuff in."

I patted my new pen in my pocket.

"Trust me on this," I said real soft.

"Well, your mittens could still turn up," he said. "Folks will surprise you sometimes."

Then he told me a story about his wallet.

"A few years ago I lost my wallet at the mall. I was sure I would never ever see it again," he said.

I bobbed my head up and down. "I

know it. That's because of *Finders keepers, losers weepers,*" I said. "*Finders keepers, losers weepers* is the rule. Right, Grampa?"

Grampa Miller smiled.

"Well, it might be the rule for *some* people," he said. "But luckily, it's not the rule for *everyone.* Because the very next day—when I went out to get my mail—there it was! My wallet was sitting right smack in the middle of my mailbox! And not one single penny was missing!"

His eyes looked happy and sparkly.

"Can you imagine that, little girl?" he asked. "Someone had the chance to take everything in my wallet. But instead, they drove all the way to my house. And they put it in my mailbox."

Just then, he reached in his back pocket and pulled out his wallet.

"Look what I would have lost if they hadn't returned it," he said.

He took a picture out of his wallet. And handed it to me.

"It's you and a baby," I said.

"But that's not just *any* baby," he said. "That's *you,* Junie B.! That's a picture of the very first time I ever held you."

He took the picture back and stared and stared at it.

"Nicest thing a stranger ever did for me...bringing this picture back," he whispered real soft.

Then he leaned over again.

And he kissed me on my head.

7
The Pink Fluffy Girl

After I talked to my grampa, I went to my room.

I closed my door real secret.

Then I took my wonderful pen out of my pocket. And I did a big sigh.

'Cause I had confusion in me, that's why.

"I wish I never even heard that wallet story," I said. "'Cause *Finders keepers, losers weepers* isn't the rule, apparently. And so now maybe I might be a crook."

I looked at my wonderful pen.

"Yeah, only I don't even *feel* like a crook. I feel like a lucky duck. But I still have to take this thing to the Lost and Found, probably. And then it will go to waste just like the teddy backpack."

All of a sudden, I heard Mother and Daddy come home from work.

I quick hided my pen under my mattress. 'Cause those two would not be understanding of this situation.

They came in my room and kissed me hello.

I told them what happened to my mittens.

Then I begged and begged for them to take me to the store. But Mother said *there's no more left*. And Daddy said *there's no more left*, too. And so there was no more left, apparently.

That's how come I got depressed all over again. And I couldn't even sleep good that night.

I kept on wondering about who was the mitten crook. And what did he look like. 'Cause I've seen crooks on TV before. And they are biggish and meanish with tattoos on theirselves.

Just then, I sat up in my bed.

'Cause a good idea popped into my head, that's why!

"Hey, a tattoo is easy to spot, I bet!" I said. "And so maybe I can find that crook on the playground tomorrow!"

After that, I went right straight to sleep. 'Cause I would need my strength for crook-looking.

The next day at recess, I didn't play

horses with Lucille and that Grace.

Instead, I runned all around the playground looking for the mitten crook.

Only too bad for me. 'Cause most of the children had their jackets on. And so I couldn't even see any crooks with tattoos.

Pretty soon, the bell rang.

That is when my eyes got tears in them. 'Cause I would never see my mittens again. Not ever, ever, never.

I started walking to Room Nine.

My nose was sniffling and drippity.

I wiped it on my attractive jacket sleeve.

Then—all of a sudden—a pink fluffy girl skipped past me.

She had on a pink fluffy dress. With pink fluffy socks and shoes. And a pink fluffy jacket made of pink fluffy fur.

And guess what else?

SHE HAD BLACK FURRY MITTENS IN HER PINK FLUFFY POCKETS!

My eyes got big and wide!

"HEY! MY MITTENS! MY MITTENS! MY MITTENS!" I screamed real loud.

Then I put my head down. And I zoomed at her like a speeding bull.

Mrs. saw me running. She grabbed me by my attractive winter jacket.

I jumped up and down and pointed.

"THAT PINK FLUFFY GIRL STOLED MY MITTENS! SHE IS THE CROOK! ONLY HER JACKET IS COVERING UP HER TATTOO! AND SO THAT'S WHAT HAD ME STUMPED!"

Mrs. called to the pink fluffy girl.

She skipped over to where we were.

I kept on jumping.

"YOU STOLED THEM! YOU STOLED MY MITTENS!" I said.

"No, I didn't," she said back. "I didn't steal anything. I *found* these mittens. They

were right in the grass. And so I thought nobody wanted them."

"I did!" I yelled. "I wanted them! My grampa Miller bought them for no good reason. And I have been worrying about them all day. And all night. And that is called heartache, madam!"

Mrs. said to hush my voice.

She took my mittens away from the pink fluffy girl. And gave them back to me.

Then she bended down. And she talked to the pink fluffy girl real serious.

"Even if you thought no one wanted these mittens, it was wrong of you to take them," she told her.

The pink fluffy girl pointed at me.

"But she didn't even take good care of them," she said.

I stamped my foot.

"Yes, I did! I did too take care of them! I left them with my attractive winter jacket. 'Cause I didn't even know there was crooks at this place!"

Mrs. said *hush* to me again.

"You should have taken them to the Lost and Found," she told the pink fluffy girl.

"Yeah! 'Cause then I would have found them when I looked there!" I said. "And so what do you think that box is there for? My health?"

The pink fluffy girl started to cry.

"But I really, really love them," she said.

Mrs. smoothed her hair.

"I'm afraid that's not the issue," she said.

"Yeah, we're afraid that's not the issue," I said. "'Cause *Finders keepers* isn't the rule, apparently. And so from now on, if you find my stuff, you have to take it to the Lost and Found. Plus also you can put it in my grampa's mailbox."

Mrs. looked at me a real long time.

She said I am getting on her nerves.

After that, she held the pink fluffy girl's hand. And they went to talk to her teacher.

I quick put my mittens on.

Then I buried my face in their black furry fur.

And I danced around real joyful.

8
I Am Not a Crook

The next day, I went to Principal's office.

The grouchy typing lady looked over the counter at me.

I rocked back and forth on my feet.

"Yeah, only I'm not even bad, again," I said. "I just need to go to the Lost and Found, and that's all."

The grouchy typing lady opened up the closet. She pulled out the big box.

Just then, the phone rang. And she hurried up to answer it.

I quick bended down and digged my hands in the Lost and Found.

Then my heart got very thrilled. 'Cause I saw that wonderful teddy backpack again, that's why!

I snuggled my face in his tummy.

"Mmm...I still love this softy guy," I whispered.

I put him on my back and skipped all around.

The grouchy typing lady hanged up the phone.

"Did you lose that, too?" she asked me. "Is that why you're here?"

I kept on standing there and standing there.

"Wellll?" she said.

Finally, I did a big sigh.

Then I walked very slow back to the box.

And I took off the teddy backpack.

"No," I said. "Not why."

After that, I reached in my pocket. And I pulled out my wonderful pen.

"I found this," I said. "It was on the

floor by the water fountain. And I really, really love it. Only that is not the issue."

Then I did a big, deep breath. And I dropped my wonderful pen into the Lost and Found.

"I am not a crook," I said kind of quiet.

The grouchy typing lady looked nicer at me. She ruffled my hair.

"No," she said. "Of course you're not a crook."

After that, I rocked back and forth on my feet some more. And I waited and waited and waited and waited.

The typing lady raised up her eyebrows at me.

"I'm waiting for the grin," I explained. "Only there seems to be a delay."

She laughed right out loud.

That's when I felt it.

The grin.

It came right on my face!

"Hey! It's working! It's working!" I said real squealy.

I skipped all around the office very happy.

Then the typing lady opened up the door. And I skipped all the way to Room Nine.

And guess what?

I didn't even find a pen that writes four different colors!

And that was a big relief!

Laugh yourself silly with

ALL the Junie B. Jones books!

Don't miss this next book about my fun in kindergarten!

Junie B. is going to a slumber party, and it is sure to be a dream come true! 'Cause what could possibly go wrong?

Available Now!

Junie B. has a lot to say
about everything and everybody . . .

the baby's room

Mother and Daddy fixed up a room for the new baby. It's called a nursery. Except I don't know why. Because a baby isn't a nurse, of course.

• from *Junie B. Jones and a Little Monkey Business*

school words

After that, the mop got removed from us. *Removed* is the school word for snatched right out of our hands.

• from *Junie B. Jones and Her Big Fat Mouth*

rules

Me and Mother had a little talk. It was called—*no screaming back off, clown.* Only I never even heard of that rule before.

• from *Junie B. Jones and the Yucky Blucky Fruitcake*

her baby brother

His name is Ollie. I love him a real lot. Except I wish he didn't live at my actual house.

• from *Junie B. Jones and That Meanie Jim's Birthday*

. . . in Barbara Park's

Junie B. Jones books!

saving a seat

Saving a seat is when you zoom on the bus. And you hurry up and sit down. And then you quick put your feet on the seat next to you. After that, you keep on screaming the word "SAVED! SAVED! SAVED!" And no one even sits next to you. 'Cause who wants to sit next to a screamer? That's what I would like to know.

• from *Junie B. Jones Loves Handsome Warren*

twirling

I twirled and twirled all over the kitchen. Only too bad for me. 'Cause I accidentally twirled into the refrigerator and the stove and the dishwasher.

• from *Junie B. Jones Is a Beauty Shop Guy*

cribs

A crib is a bed with bars on the side of it. It's kind of like a cage at the zoo. Except with a crib, you can put your hand through the bars. And the baby won't pull you in and kill you.

• from *Junie B. Jones and a Little Monkey Business*